STAR PLAYER

JENNIFER MAHARAJH

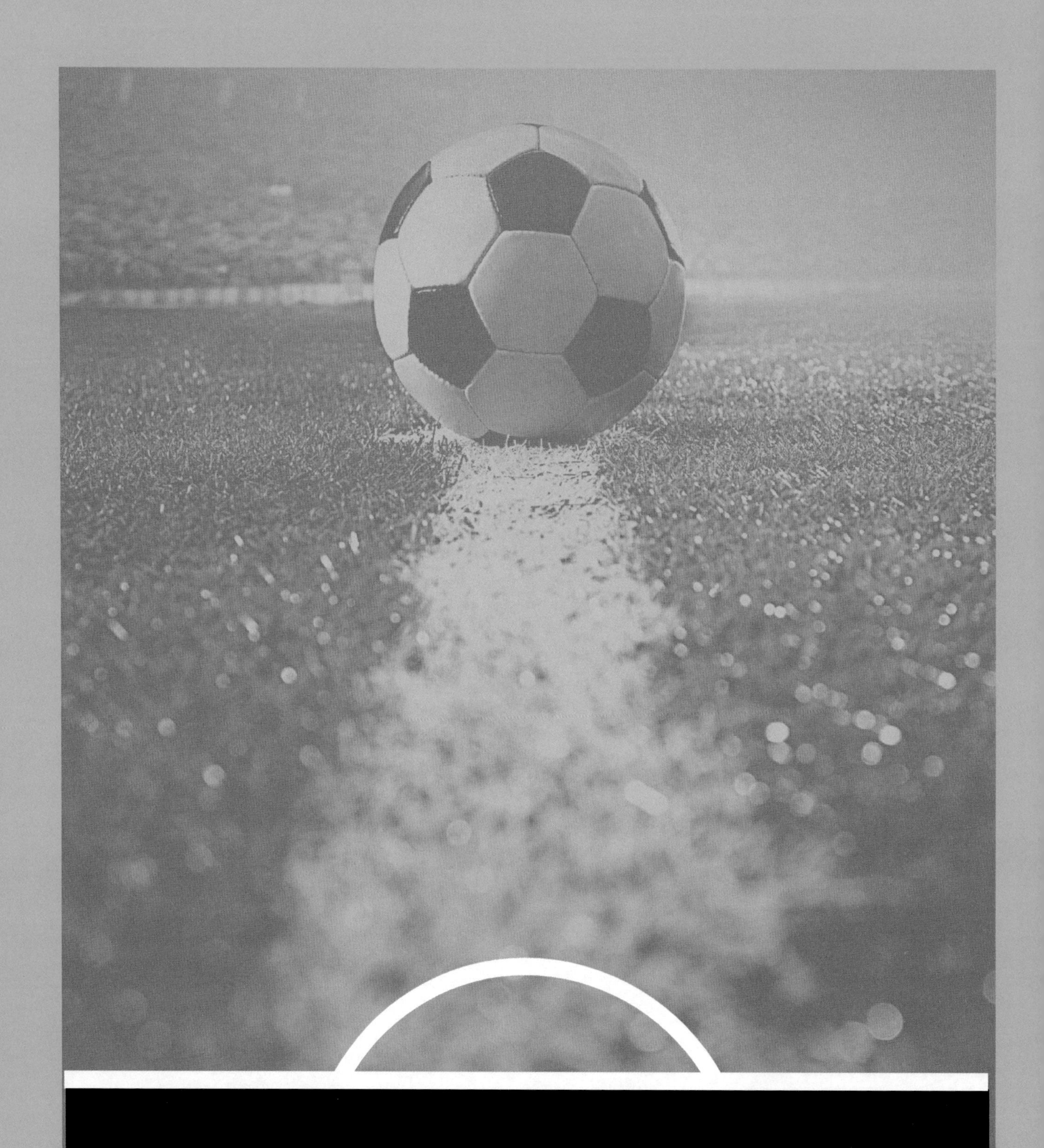

Dedicated to the Boston Boys

Bradley, Nicholas and Dylan

This is a work of fiction. Names, characters, places, and incidents either are the product of the author's imagination or are used fictitiously. Any resemblance to actual persons, living or dead, events, or locales is entirely coincidental.

First Paperback edition March 2021

ISBN 9798713894597

Independent Publishing

www.simplysignaturebooks.com

"Let's go gang, hustle hustle!" shouted Coach Gerry.

"Move those feet, keep control and let's win this game boys."

Bradley picked up speed and kicked and turned and ran down the field as quickly as his little legs could carry him.

The mid afternoon sun hovered over the field hiding the shade.

He was so hot he could feel his shirt sticking to his belly. His cleats squished on the grass. He quickly wiped away the sweat with his elbow.

This was the Rallycat's 4th game of the season and they were 4-0.

Bradley had been playing soccer since he was 3 years old. It was his favorite sport.

His dad signed him up for all the soccer camps and trainings and would always tell him, "as long as you have heart, spirit and sportsmanship, you're always a winner and star player."

"Go Bradley, go!"

"Score a goal so we can get ice-cream," screamed his little brother Nick from the bleachers.

Nick jumped up and threw his hands in the air.

"I want chocolate ice-cream with sprinkles!" he shouted.

Nick was 5 years old and baseball was his favorite sport, but he always liked to watch Bradley's games.

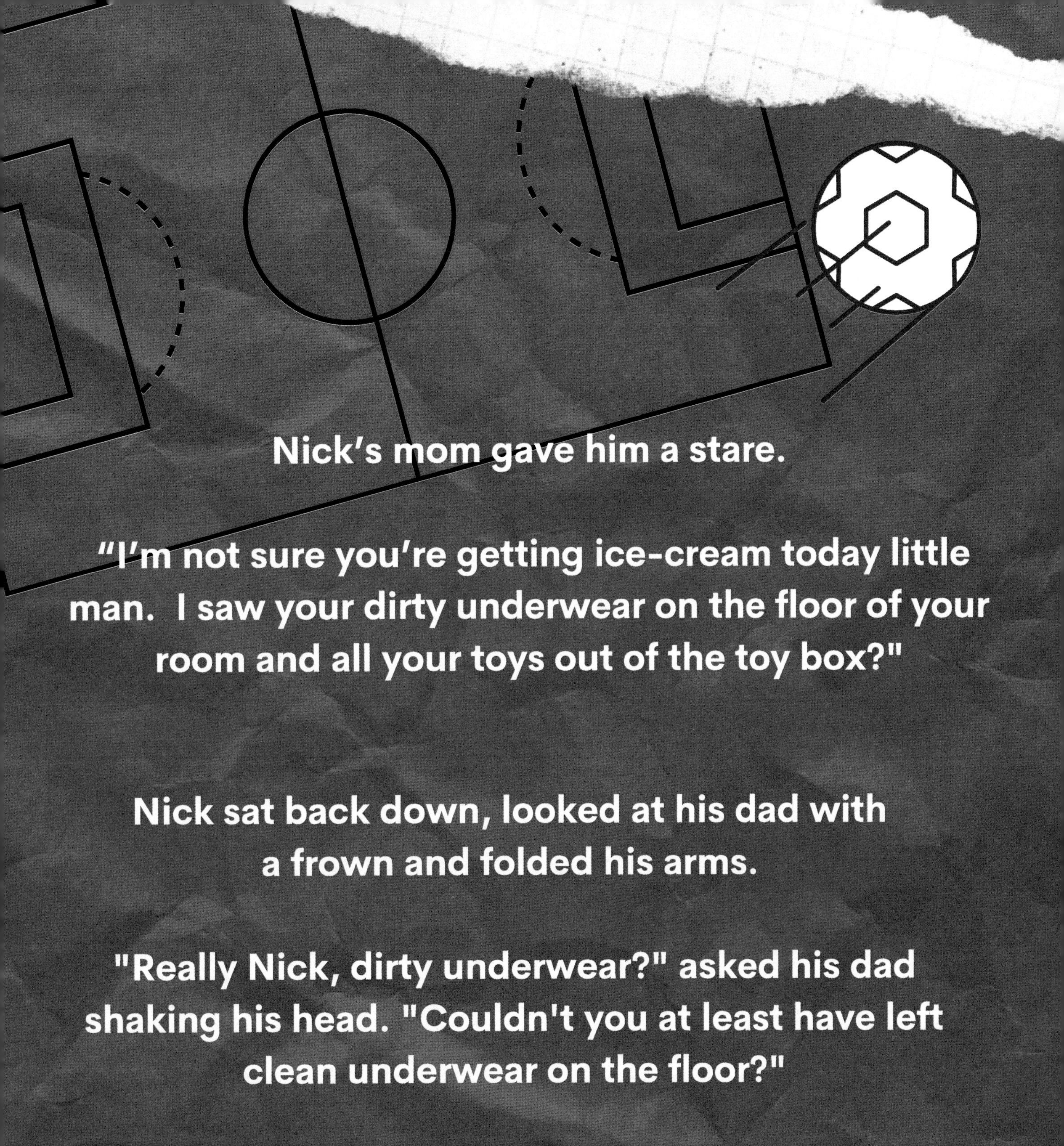

Nick’s mom gave him a stare.

“I’m not sure you’re getting ice-cream today little man. I saw your dirty underwear on the floor of your room and all your toys out of the toy box?"

Nick sat back down, looked at his dad with a frown and folded his arms.

"Really Nick, dirty underwear?" asked his dad shaking his head. "Couldn't you at least have left clean underwear on the floor?"

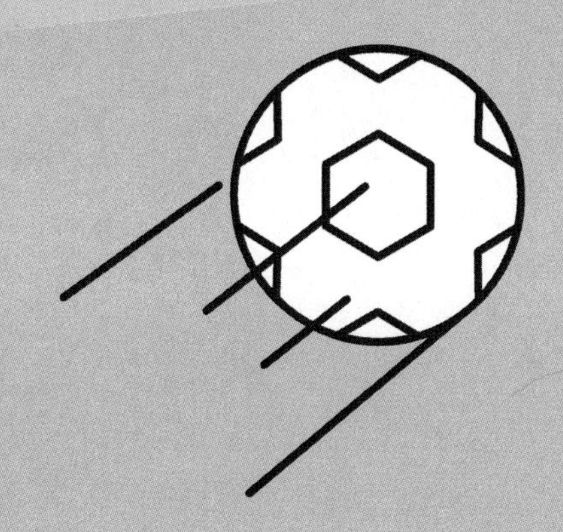

He gave Nick a friendly punch in the shoulder and whispered in his ears, "Tell mom it was Dylan."

Nick's face lit up. "Mom, mom, I forgot it was Dylan. He came into my room while I was asleep and took my underwear out of the hamper and knocked over all my toys!"

Marsha raised her eyebrows at Nick and glanced over at 6-month-old Dylan chewing on a rubber zebra.

Jon smiled and high-fived Nick. "See, told you that would work."

Score!

Bradley got the first goal of the game!

Marsha, Jon and Nick all jumped off the bleachers chorusing, "Bradley, Bradley, Bradley!"

Bradley gave his family a thumbs up.

He looked back at the field. The Midnitewolves looked so bummed, especially Timothy.

Timothy had been playing just as long as Bradley and they were always competing.

"Okay team, heads up and eyes on the ball," shouted Coach.

Marcus passed the ball to Bradley. Bradley jumped into action and moved into position.

Then, Bradley spotted Timothy.

He was coming towards him full speed with wide eyes and quick feet. He was close, real close.

Bradley could see the goal. Could he make it? He turned left, he shot around to his right cutting the ball in and out.

Bradley planted his feet and set in motion the drop kick his dad taught him.

Timothy was ready too. He went for a tackle and blocked Bradley's drop kick.

BANG!

Timothy's cleats collided into Bradley's knee. He heard the pop. Bradley felt a stinging pain all the way up his leg. He fell to the floor, tears streaming down his face.

Jon jumped off the bleachers and quickly rushed out to the field.

Marsha in a panic nervously grabbed Nick and Dylan.

Coach Gerry and the team surrounded Bradley. He sat in pain grasping his knee tightly.

Timothy stared in shock. He didn't mean to hurt him. He felt really bad.

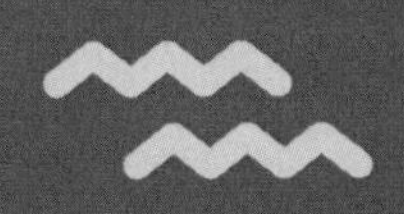

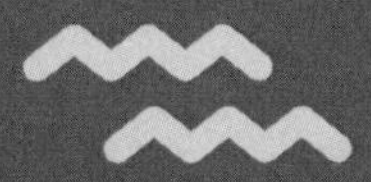

The next morning, Bradley sat sulking on the couch with his leg stretched out on a soft pillow.

The doctor said it was a torn ligament and he would be out for the rest of the season.

To an 8 year old, that felt like forever.

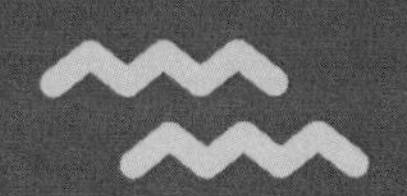

"Hey pal, how about some pancakes with bananas and whip cream?" asked his mom.

"Sure, why not. I'll be stuck here forever anyways. Might as while eat. Can you add a glass of chocolate milk too?"

His mom smiled. "I think forever sounds a little long. You"ll be back on the field in no time. You just need to heal that knee."

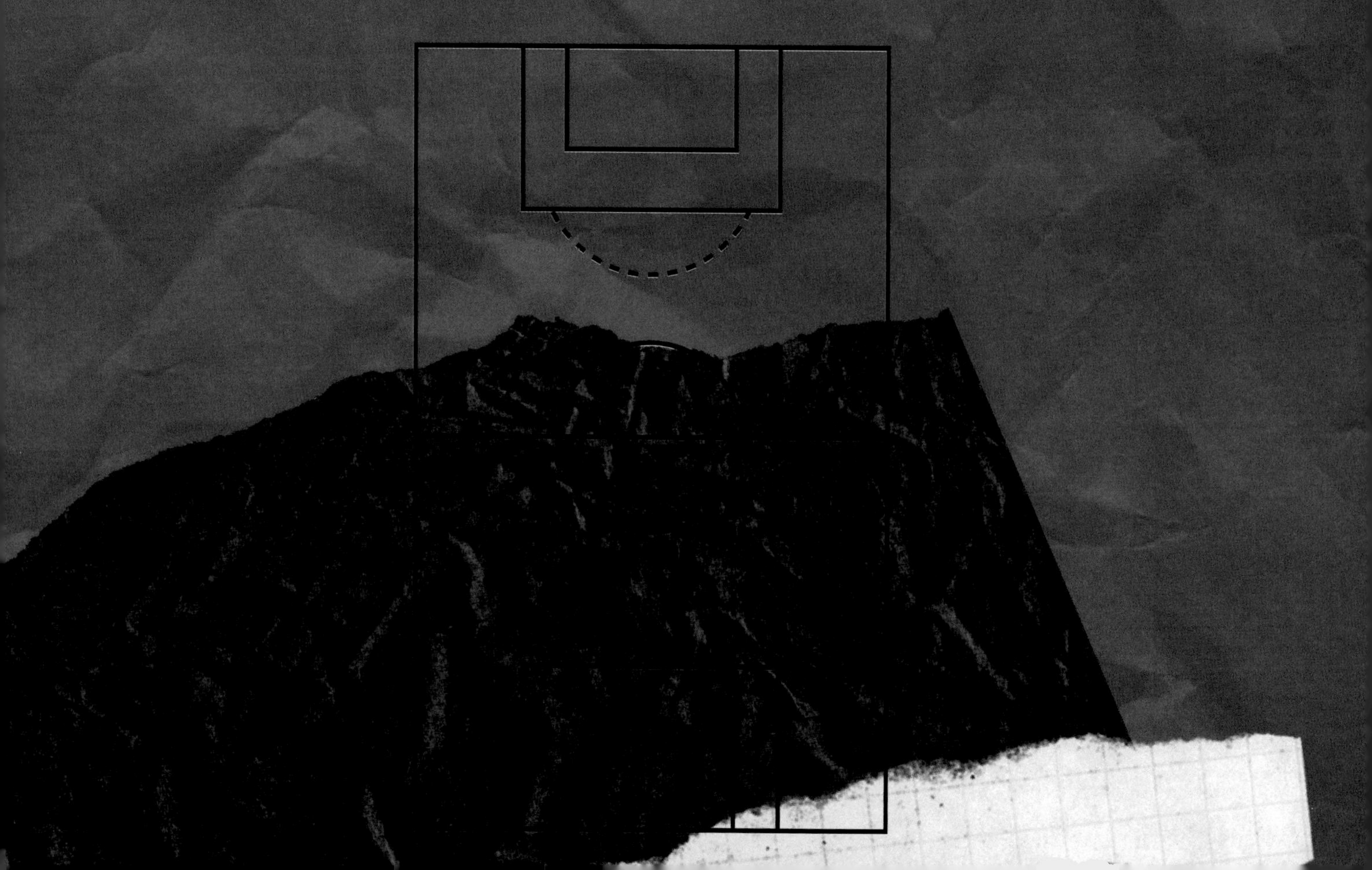

“I can’t believe that Timothy.
He gets to play and I don’t."

"He gets to go to the annual soccer picnic too."

"I’ll never forgive him, never!”
shouted Bradley folding his arms.

Bradley's outburst interrupted Nick.

“Bradley, be quiet, shouted back
Nick. I’m watching TV.” Bradley gave
his little brother a dirty look.

Jon walked over to Bradley and sat down beside him.

"I know you're upset, but you can't be angry forever."

"Why not? He tackled me, hurt my knee and now I can't play soccer or ride my bike."

"It was an accident. Sometimes people do things they don't mean. Plus, you'll be playing again real soon."

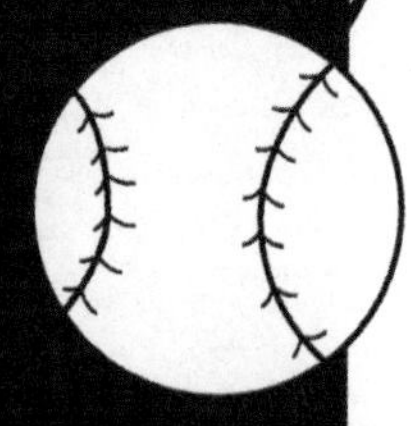

"Yeah, but I'll miss so much. It's all his fault!"

"Remember when you accidentally threw mom's watch in the sink that Grandpa gave her?"

Bradley slumped down on the couch. He surely did remember. His mom wasn't happy.

"Well, didn't mom tell you it was okay and she forgives you?"

"Yeah, but she's my mom, she has too."

"What if she told you she was still angry, wouldn't that hurt your feelings?"

Bradley nodded. "Yeah I guess," he said with a frown.

"You have to let go of your anger and move past it."

"How do I let go of it?" asked Bradley. "I can't forget what happened."

"Not forget, but forgive," said his dad. "You can be strong inside and not think about those angry feelings anymore."

"Bradley, whatever happened on the soccer field, happened yesterday. Today is a new day. You can choose how you want to feel today."

"Also, you can talk to Timothy and let him know how you feel," said Jon.

"So, I tell him I'm mad and how much my knee hurts? I tell him that it's not fair he gets to play and I don't?"

"Yes, exactly. It's important to let out your feelings when you're angry. If you keep them bottled up, you can explode at the wrong time."

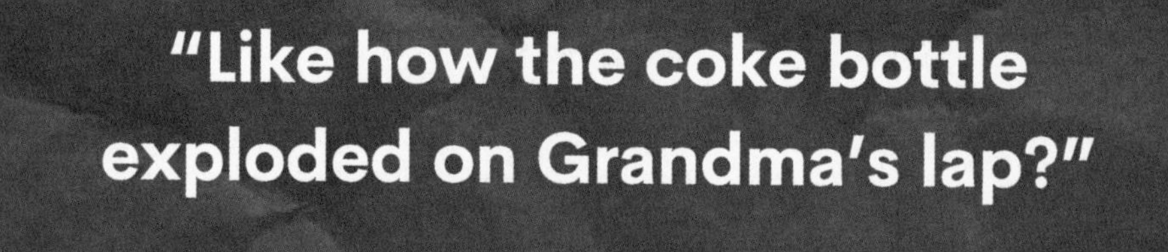

"Like how the coke bottle exploded on Grandma's lap?"

Bradley laughed. "That was funny dad!"

Jon smiled "Yes, like the coke bottle exploding on Grandma's lap."

He thought it was funny too, but his mother didn't think so.

"Forgiving Timothy has to be your choice Bradley."

"Mom and I won't force you to do anything. But you will feel so much better if you do."

"It takes strength and courage to forgive someone. Forgiveness shows kindness and I know you're a kind little boy."

"Being a star player is important on and off the field."

Nick came running up to Bradley.

"Bradley, I forgive you for yelling when I was watching TV," he said as he threw himself on his brother's belly.

Bradley and his dad burst into laughter.

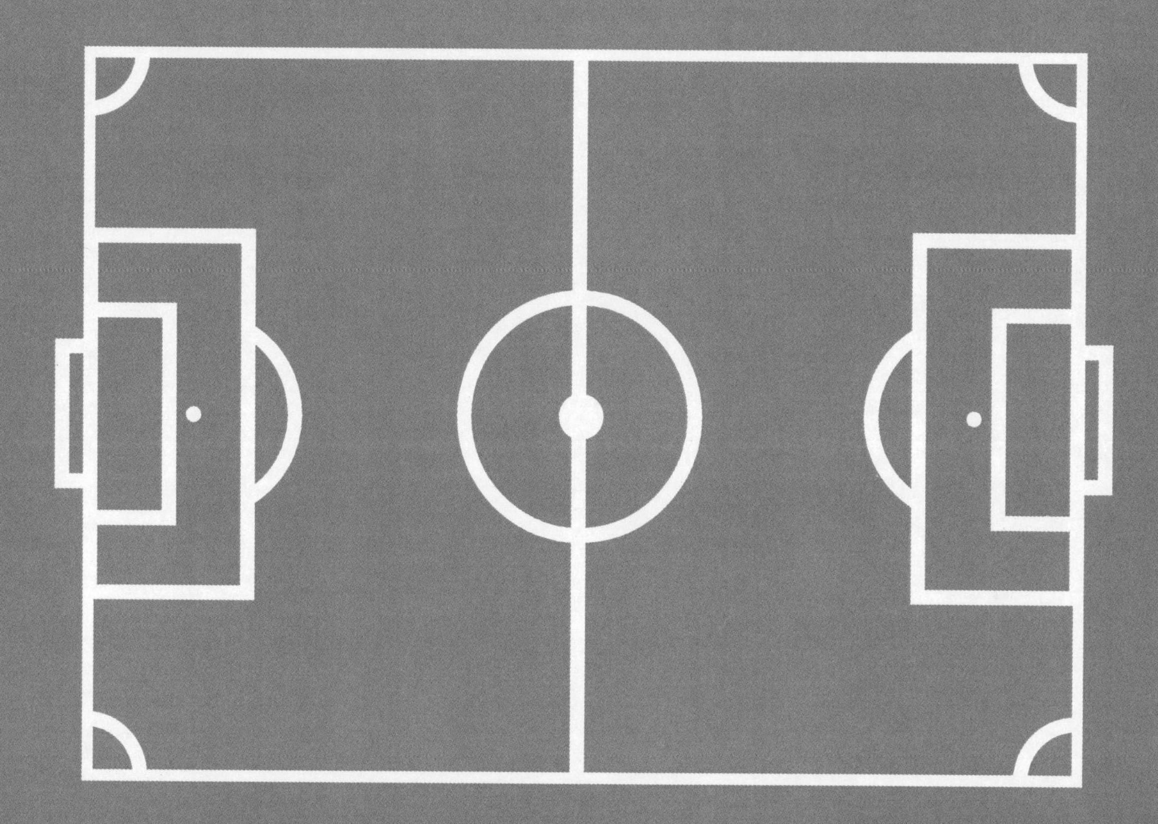

The next weekend Bradley and his dad went to watch his team play.

"Hey champ, how's the knee?" asked Coach Gerry patting Bradley on his back.

"Good, how's the team without me?"

Coach Gerry laughed. "Why don't you hop on over and go ask them yourself."

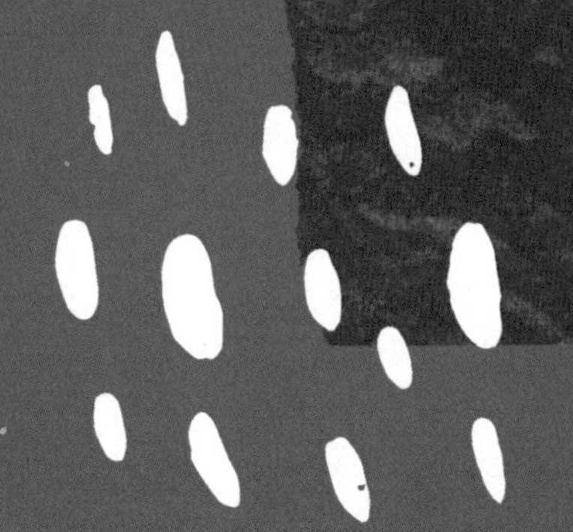

Bradley made his way over to his teammates who were super excited to see him. As they talked and laughed, Bradley watched them do warm up drills.

Bradley felt a tap on his shoulder. “Hi Bradley,” said Timothy quietly. Bradley swung around “Hey," answered Bradley.

"How’s your knee?” “It’s okay. At least I get to sit on the couch and watch TV all day."

Timothy laughed. "I'm jealous."

“I’m sorry Bradley, I didn’t mean to hurt you. I guess I need to practice my tackle a little more."

Bradley glanced over at his father.
Jon smiled at his son and nodded.

“I know Timothy, it’s okay.
Maybe we can practice together."

Timothy’s face lit up.
He and Bradley shook hands.

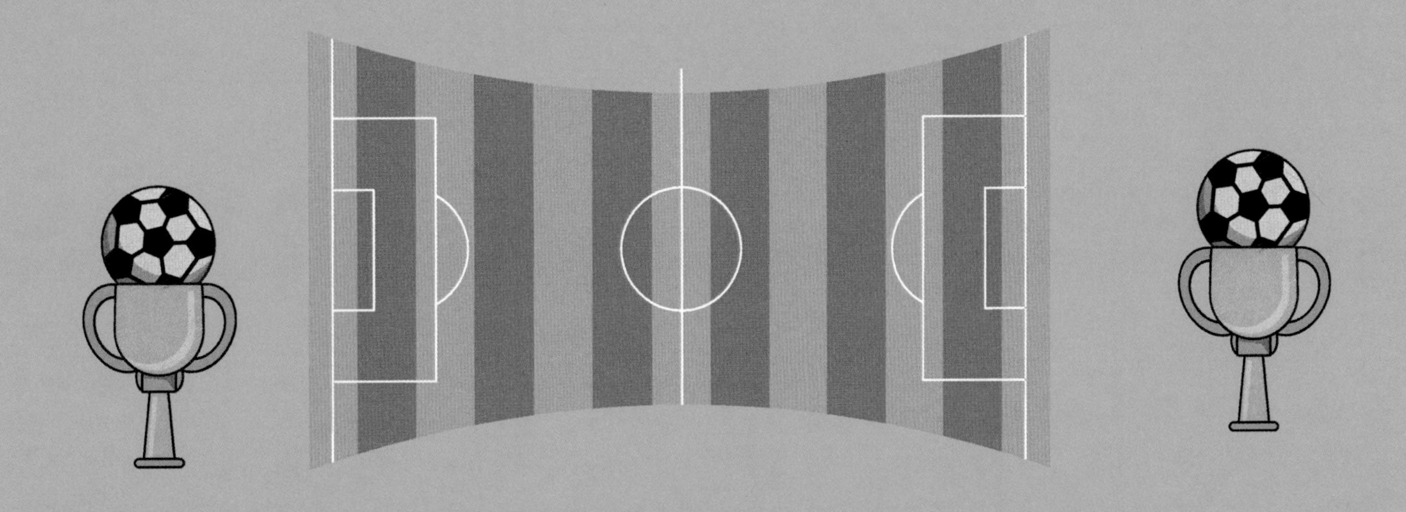

Bradley missed the rest of the season, but was back on the soccer field a few weeks later practicing his drop kick.

Timothy joined him to practice his tackle. They now practice together twice a week.

Steps to Forgive

Let go of anger

Move Past it

Forgive and show kindness

What are some things you can do if you feel sad or angry at someone?

I imagine life just the way it is. I create the outcome of my life by believing in me. I live my life with confidence and positive thoughts. This is how I write.

Writing is my therapeutic passion. I am so grateful to create, and bring to life my thoughts and imagination. Life has certainly brought me challenges, but also the opportunity to embrace new beginnings, learn, grow and keep achieving.

My two beautiful daughters continue to inspire me each and every day.

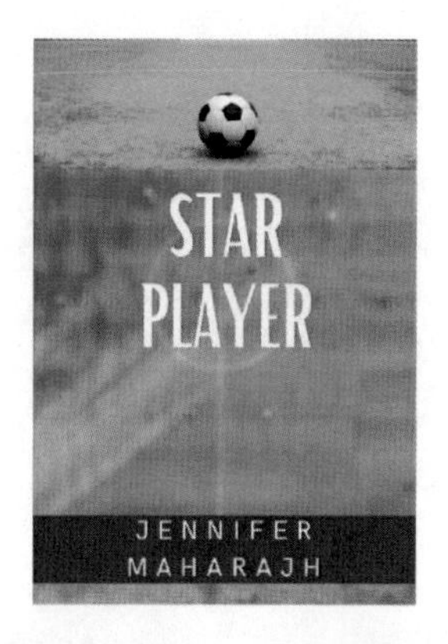

www.simplysignaturebooks.com

Made in the USA
Middletown, DE
21 April 2021